Sonny

Saddle Up Series
Book 54

Dave and Pat Sargent are longtime residents of Prairie Grove, Arkansas. Dave, a fourth-generation dairy farmer, began writing in early December of 1990. Pat, a former teacher, began writing in the fourth grade. They enjoy the outdoors and have a real love for animals.

Sonny

Saddle Up Series
Book 54

By Dave and Pat Sargent

Beyond "The End"
By Sue Rogers

Illustrated by Jane Lenoir

Ozark Publishing, Inc.
P.O. Box 228
Prairie Grove, AR 72753

Cataloging-in-Publication Data

Sargent, Dave, 1941–
    Sonny / by Dave and Pat Sargent ; illustrated
by Jane Lenoir.—Prairie Grove, AR :
Ozark Publishing, c2004.
    p. cm. (Saddle up series ; 54)

    "Have orderly manners"—Cover.
    SUMMARY: Sonny, a horse belonging
to Bat Masterson in Deadwood, South Dakota,
helps capture an outlaw. Contains factual
information about linebacked yellow dun horses.
    ISBN 1-56763-715-9 (hc)
            1-56763-716-7 (pbk
)
    1. Horses—Juvenile fiction. [1. Horses—
Fiction. 2. Masterson, Bat, 1853–1921—Fiction.]
I. Sargent, Pat, 1936– II. Lenoir, Jane, 1950– ill.
III. Title. IV. Series.

    PZ10.3.S243So 2004
    [Fic]—dc21   2001005628

Printed in the United States of America

iv

Inspired by

linebacked yellow duns we see in this beautiful country we live in.

Dedicated to

all children
with pale yellow hair.

Foreword

Sonny is a linebacked yellow dun. He lives in South Dakota, in the town of Deadwood, where gold has just been discovered. His new boss, Bat Masterson, takes him to Dodge City, Kansas, where he plans to run for sheriff of Ford County.

Contents

If you would like to have the authors of the Saddle Up Series visit your school, free of charge, call 1-800-321-5671 or 1-800-960-3876.

One

Bat Masterson

Deadwood, South Dakota, was bustling with activity. A feeling of excitement rushed through Sonny the linebacked yellow dun as he watched other horses, burros, and people travel up and down the dusty street. "Hmmm," he thought. "This is one busy town. I wonder what all of the fuss is about."

A man came out of an office with a piece of paper in his hand. Sonny watched as he nailed it onto a post.

"This hombre right here is a wanted man," he said as he pointed to the face on the poster. "There's a five-hundred-dollar reward for the one who captures him."

The linebacked yellow dun stared at the picture of the outlaw for several seconds.

"Wow!" he finally nickered. "He has robbed stagecoaches and banks and little old ladies. He has also stolen from trains and shops and little old men. In the first place, he's very busy. In the second place, he's a very nasty person. I'd sure like to catch him," he snorted. A moment later, he added, "Unless I'm badly mistaken, my livery boss could sure use that big reward."

Several minutes later, Sonny wandered over to a big shade tree to watch the town's newcomers go by.

"Hi, stranger," he nickered to a silver grullo who was walking up the main street. "What brings you to Deadwood?"

"Howdy," the silver grullo said. "Folks found gold. Isn't that why you're here?"

"No," Sonny said with a smile. "I've lived here since I was a colt. But it was never this busy."

"You better get used to it," the grullo said with a chuckle. "Because gold fever makes folks kind of loco. My boss loves to hunt for gold, and we move every time somebody finds a new mother lode someplace else."

"Sounds like an exciting life," Sonny said. "Good luck to you."

"Hmmm," Sonny thought as he stepped out of the way for a bearded man and a burro to pass. "It sounds like my quiet life in Deadwood is over."

"This is good!" he neighed. "I'm ready for some excitement."

Five nights later, Sonny heard a noise in the livery stable where he was sleeping.

"Oh no," he groaned. "I hope it isn't that nasty guy on the wanted poster." He thought for a second, then added, "He wouldn't rob me anyway. I don't have anything but a flake of hay and a halter." The linebacked yellow dun sighed as a man walked up to him.

"What's happening tonight, Stable Boss?" he asked. "What are you doing up so late?"

"I'm sorry, Sonny," the fellow said. "I did a real bad thing tonight. I used you for my bet in a poker game."

"What?" the linebacked yellow dun whinnied. "How could you gamble me away like that, Boss? I'm not a poker chip!"

"I'm truly sorry, Sonny," the livery man said sadly. "But I was positive that I would win, and you'd have all the oats you wanted for the rest of your life."

"Humph!" Sonny said with a snort. "A horse does not live on oats alone. A stable home life is very important, too!"

He followed the man from the livery stable. "Oh mercy," he thought. "What's going to happen to me now? This new-boss business is kind of scary." A well-dressed man was waiting for them at the hitching post. He smiled at Sonny.

"Wow! I think he likes me!" Sonny exclaimed. "He looks like he may be an okay boss."

The livery stable man handed the linebacked yellow dun's halter rope to his new boss.

"Sonny is a special horse," the man said sadly. "I'd appreciate it if you'd take extra good care of him, Mr. Masterson."

"Humph!" Sonny snorted again. "You better tell me to take care of this gambling man."

The well-dressed man doffed his hat and said, "Don't worry, Sir. Sonny will have a good home. We'll be going to Dodge City, Kansas. I've decided to try for the position of Ford County sheriff."

"Hey," Sonny nickered, "that sounds like an exciting life, Boss. Let's go!"

The sun was bright and cheerful the following morning as Sonny and Bat walked away from Deadwood.

"I'm sure going to miss my old friends," Sonny thought. "But life in Dodge City sounds like fun. I hope Boss wins that sheriff thing he just mentioned. I think it would be neat to be a lawhorse."

The linebacked yellow dun nickered farewell to his bay sabino friend and nuzzled the lilac dun on her neck as they passed.

Two

Dodge City, Kansas

The journey from South Dakota was beautiful and interesting for Sonny the linebacked yellow dun. With each passing day, he learned more and more about his new boss. Bat Masterson was friendly and nice to everyone they met.

"You're a real fun guy, Boss," he whinnied. "I think we're going to be a good team."

Bat patted him on the shoulder and asked, "Will it be okay with you if we stop in Cripple Creek for a day or two, Sonny? I've heard some good things about that mining town. We may as well have some fun on the way to Dodge City. When I become a sheriff, we're going to have to work instead of play."

"That's a real good idea, Boss," Sonny agreed. "Let's have some fun before we go to work."

But only moments later, after he'd had time to think about it, he groaned and then shook his head. "Maybe we better not stop in that Cripple Creek town in Colorado. I heard they do a lot of gambling there, and I don't want to be used for a poker chip anymore."

Slowly reining Sonny to a halt, Bat swung his leg over the back of the saddle and stepped down. He stroked Sonny on his nose.

"My friend," he said with a chuckle, "you're tense. I bet you're worried that I'm going to lose you in a poker game, aren't you?"

A tear slowly trickled from one eye as the linebacked yellow dun nodded his head.

"Sonny, you and I are partners," Bat said in a serious tone of voice. "I'll never use you to cover one of my bets. We're friends and partners. Don't you agree?"

"I am one lucky horse, Boss," the linebacked yellow dun whinnied. "We're going to have wonderful and exciting times together. Let's go to Cripple Creek!"

The town of Cripple Creek was a lot like Deadwood. There were horses, burros, and folks bustling all up and down the streets, gathering the supplies they would need to look for gold in the Rocky Mountains. They had to take enough supplies to last for months since they wouldn't be able to come into town very often. Sonny visited with the local horses while Bat enjoyed the people.

One evening while Sonny was standing at the hitching post in front of the hotel, a familiar-looking man walked out the door. "Hmmm," the linebacked yellow dun thought. "I should know that fellow." Suddenly his foretop stood straight up.

"Good grief!" he nickered in a loud voice. "That's him! That's the man on the wanted poster."

The outlaw glared at Sonny, but then he turned and walked down the boardwalk toward the livery stable.

Sonny hurried to the window of the hotel and peeked inside. Bat was shuffling a deck of cards as he laughed and talked.

"Hey, Boss!" Sonny whispered hoarsely. "Come out here. We have work to do."

A moment later, Bat noticed Sonny nudging his nose against the windowpane, but he motioned for the horse to leave.

"But, Boss," Sonny pleaded, "the bad guy is going to get away."

Bat glared at the linebacked yellow dun and again motioned for

him to leave. Sonny slowly backed
away from the window.

"Now what am I going to do?" he murmured. "Boss just doesn't understand that we have important business with that outlaw."

A second later, he knew what he had to do. He turned and trotted briskly toward the livery stable. The outlaw was leading a linebacked claybank dun horse through the door when he arrived.

"Is this man your boss?" Sonny asked the claybank dun.

"No, he's not." Then he added, "My boss is Wyatt Earp. I don't know why this guy saddled me. My boss is at the hotel."

Sonny quickly told him about the wanted poster that he had seen in Deadwood a few days ago.

"Wow!" Wyatt Earp's horse exclaimed. "What should we do?"

For a brief moment, Sonny bit his lip and tapped one hoof on the ground. Then suddenly his ears shot forward.

"Listen closely," he whispered. "I have a plan that just might capture this outlaw and give our bosses five hundred dollars."

Three

The $500.00 Reward

Fifteen minutes later, Sonny quietly followed the claybank dun and the outlaw away from town.

As they approached a large tree with low branches, Sonny nickered, "Now, friend! Come uncorked!"

The head of the claybank dun went down, and his hind legs flew up. He snorted and bucked and reared until the outlaw lost his grip and soared through the air. Sonny jerked the rope from the saddle and ran over to the man who was now sprawled on the ground. As luck would have it, the loop dropped over the man's shoulders as he sat up.

"Now, run around him, Sonny! Hurry! " the linebacked claybank dun neighed. "You've got him! Wrap that rope around him."

Sonny did just that. He ran around and around the outlaw until he had him tied up good and tight.

By the time the two horses neared the town, they had become good friends. They had learned to respect each other and they admired each other.

Within a very short time, the linebacked yellow dun and the line-backed claybank dun walked back into Cripple Creek. They got lots of attention from the folks on the street because the outlaw was at the end of a long rope, following them. The horses looked at each other as they stopped in front of the hotel.

"Boss!" Sonny nickered loudly. "We need your help to turn this guy over to the sheriff."

The claybank dun stomped his front hoof on the ground and yelled, "Come on, Boss. You and Sonny's boss have some reward money to collect."

People were pointing fingers and laughing at the comical sight. Then folks hurried out of the hotel to see what all the commotion was about. Finally Sonny saw his boss walking through the crowd with a tall fellow.

"That's my boss," Sonny said proudly.

"Hmmm," the claybank dun murmured. "He's walking with my boss. They must know each other."

"That's great!" Sonny nickered.

"I found a new friend. Boss found a new friend. And we all found an outlaw worth five hundred dollars."

The next day, Bat was saddling Sonny when Wyatt Earp walked into the livery stable. As the men visited, Sonny and the claybank dun talked together.

"It sounds like we both have bosses who are lawmen," Sonny said proudly.

"It also sounds like we'll be going to Dodge City with you and your boss," the claybank dun said. "Things are really picking up in my life! Not that it's ever boring with Boss Wyatt."

"Wow-wee!" Sonny exclaimed. "Life just seems to be getting better and better."

The journey from the town of Cripple Creek was exciting for the two horses as they listened to Bat and Wyatt exchange funny stories and make plans for the future.

It was two weeks later when Sonny the linebacked yellow dun and Nick the linebacked claybank dun trotted into Dodge City, Kansas.

"Hmmm," Sonny thought as he watched folks welcome their bosses to town. "It sure is nice to have a boss who is respected and loved."

Sonny felt good. He beamed, watching his boss.

The linebacked yellow dun was thinking, "History books will one day tell about Bat Masterson. Folks will remember him as a fine man and a good sheriff."

Hmmm," he murmured. "I wonder if they'll remember his faithful linebacked yellow dun named Sonny. Well, I guess it really doesn't matter," he chuckled softly. "Life is wonderful and exciting in the Wild West!"

Four

Linebacked Yellow Dun Facts

Cowboys call yellow duns buckskins, but they are really horses with yellow bodies and no black points. The linebacked yellow dun has a black stripe down its back.

Yellow duns are yellow with brown points and look like zebra duns and buckskins except the points are brown instead of black.

Long ago, the palomino was a member of the yellow dun group. But some cowboys now consider palominos as a separate group.

BEYOND "THE END"

It excites me that no matter how much machinery replaces the horse, the work it can do is still measured in horsepower even in this space age. And although a riding horse often weighs half a ton, and a big drafter a full ton, either can be led about by a piece of string if he has been wisely trained. This to me is a constant source of wonder and challenge.

Marguerite Henry

WORD LIST

currycomb
linebacked yellow dun
foretop
silver grullo
halter
nickered
bay sabino

reins

sock

lilac dun

snort

linebacked claybank dun

hoof pick

Arabian

barrel

From the word list above, write:

1. One word that names a breed of horse.
2. One word that tells a mark on a horse.
3. Two words that are points of a horse.
4. Two words that are tack articles.
5. Two words that are sounds a horse makes.
6. Two words that are grooming tools.
7. Five word combinations that tell the color of a horse.

Write the description for these five horse color combinations!

CURRICULUM CONNECTIONS

What do these stripe descriptions on horses have in common—dorsal, eel, and linebacked?

Was Bat Masterson a real person? What was his real name? Where was he born? Bat Masterson had many jobs. Circle the one job below that he did not have:

farmer   buffalo hunter
army scout   cattle rancher
marshal   saloonkeeper
gambler   sports writer

Learn more about Bat Masterson at website <www.mysteriesofcanada.com/Quebec/bat_masterson.htm>.

Most of the people who made the long journey to California in search of gold traveled on an established route. What was the name of this route? Many of these travelers were not prepared for the hot dry deserts of Nevada. What necessity was most scarce along the trail?

PROJECT

Combine your math and artistic skills! Draw to scale and accurately color a picture (body, tail, and mane) of the horse that is featured in each book read in the Saddle Up Series. You could soon have sixty horses prancing around the walls of your classroom!

Learning + horses = FUN.

Look in your school library media center for books about how to draw a horse and the colors of horses. Don't forget the useful information in the last chapter of this book (Linebacked Yellow Dun Facts) and the picture on the book cover for a shape and color guide.

HELPFUL HINTS AND WEBSITES

A horse is measured in hands. One hand equals four inches. Use a scale of 1" equals 1 hand. Visit website <www. equisearch.com> to find a glossary of equine terms, information about tack and equipment, breeds, art and graphics, and more about horses. Learn more at <www.horse-country. com> and at <www.ansi.okstate.edu/breeds/horses/>. KidsClick! is a web search for kids by librarians. There are many interesting websites here. HORSES and HORSE-MANSHIP are two of the more than 600 subjects. Visit <www.kidsclick.org>. Is your classroom beginning to look like the Rocking S Horse Ranch? Happy Trails to You!

ANSWERS (1. All describe a continuous stripe of black or brown hair from neck to tail. 2. Sources show two names, Bartholomew Masterson and William Barclay Masterson, and two birthplaces, Quebec or Illinois. Think about "reliable sources"! 3. Cattle rancher. 4. Oregon-California Trail. 5. Water. Some paid as much as $100 for a cup of water!)